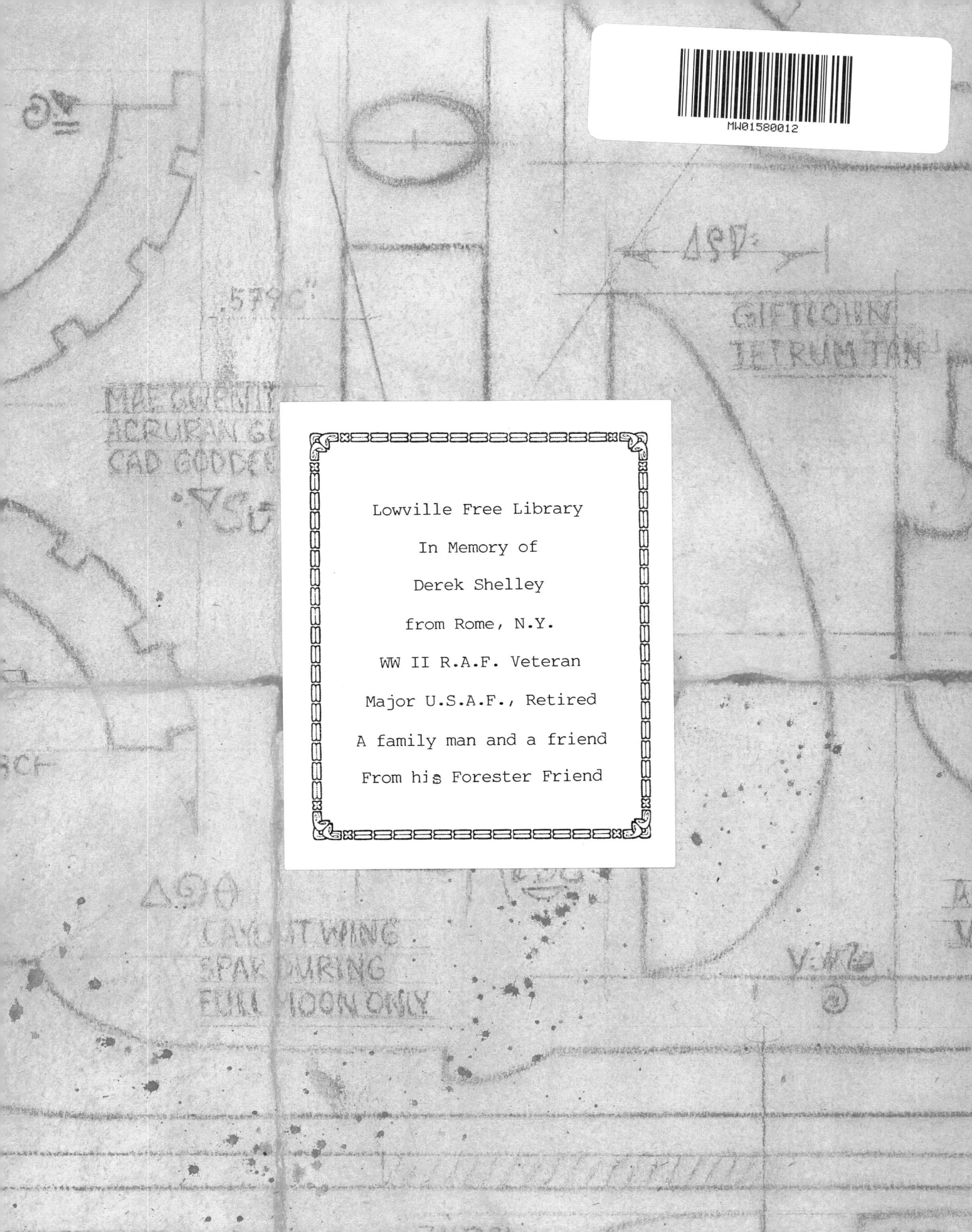

Lowville Free Library

In Memory of

Derek Shelley

from Rome, N.Y.

WW II R.A.F. Veteran

Major U.S.A.F., Retired

A family man and a friend

From his Forester Friend

Winnie·Mae

Winnie·Mae

H. B. Lewis

Creative Editions
Mankato
Harcourt Brace & Company
San Diego New York London

Ford Tri-motor

For my mom
Who has always loved to dream

For my dad
Who taught me to fly

For Levent
Who helped me to remember

And for Rachel
Who helped clear the way

Sopwith Camel

The breeze at dawn has secrets to tell you.
    Don't go back to sleep.
You must ask for what you really want.
    Don't go back to sleep.
People are going back and forth across the doorsill
    where the two worlds touch.
The door is round and open.
    Don't go back to sleep.

    —Rumi

The boy sat quietly on the porch steps, listening to the warm buzz of insects starting up all around him. Counting the minutes with an occasional toss of a pebble into the driveway, the boy waited for the world to wake up. Centuries passed as he watched the sun move up through the trees and just when he thought he couldn't sit still another moment, it was time to go. He walked his bicycle out to the road and pushed off, heading toward town and the hobby shop.

Winnie Mae

A couple of weeks ago, he finished the Sopwith Camel, a pretty difficult model. Sure it was precut, but the pieces were tiny, and stretching the tissue-paper covering was tricky business. Since then he had been working hard cutting lawns and doing odd jobs, saving every penny to buy another plane.

At the bottom of the long hill into town was a stone bridge overlooking a favorite fishing hole. The bridge was a gathering spot for the older men of the town. The boy would often make a special trip over there on Saturday mornings. He loved to sit with his feet dangling off the bridge, listening to the old men talk and watching the fishing lines drift with the current. This morning, as the boy flashed past the fishermen clustered on the bridge, he just waved briefly. The old men knew of his expedition that morning, as he had bent their ears about it for weeks. The boy rolled past, spokes winking in the sunlight, with murmured hellos and good mornings echoing in his ears as he settled into the last climb before town.

It took a few seconds for his eyes to adjust, but when he stepped down into the cool, shadowy depths of the hobby shop, he could hear

Winnie Mae

the familiar sound of Mr. Farsee's radio playing Count Basie's big band music. The boy loved to come here early on Saturdays because Mr. Farsee always respectfully left him alone to wander among the aisles and dream. Suspended from the ceiling were airplanes and dirigibles of every description. In summer the large fan in the back of the shop was always on, and as the boy wandered through the shop, the airplanes would slowly turn and dip as if they were really flying. Mr. Farsee had just received a new shipment of model kits that morning, and he held one up to show the boy. "This, my young friend, is the famous Winnie Mae. It is truly about time they made a kit for this magnificent craft." Mr. Farsee was always pleased to review the new arrivals with an appreciative audience. "This airplane was the first to be flown solo around the world. Wiley Post was the name of the pilot—a most unusual man. He only had one good eye, but managed to fly this old behemoth single-handedly around the world."

The boy hardly heard him. As soon as he saw the painting on the cover of the box, he knew it was the plane for him. He asked the price and was crushed to find it was more money than he had.

Winnie·Mae

Winnie Mae

"I'm very sorry, young man, but perhaps it's meant to be." Mr. Farsee adjusted his glasses to read the fine print on the side of the box. "It says here, for advanced seekers only."

The boy took his time on the way home. He stopped to watch a hawk wheeling gracefully overhead in the morning air and squinted up into the blue, wondering what it would be like to move in and out of the clouds. It was strange how sure he had felt about that model. It seemed so right for him and yet he couldn't afford it. Maybe it was an "extravagance." His parents used that word often, and always to point out something that was unnecessary.

Three days later, Mrs. Cranston from next door called and asked if the boy could help clean out her basement, and then the Morriseys hired him to weed their garden and mow their lawn. It was odd, but by the end of the week, he had exactly enough money to buy the kit! He had built a Curtis Jenny that hung in his room, and had done not too bad a job on a Ford Tri-motor with a little help from his dad. The Sopwith Camel was hard going, but he had built that one all by himself. He fanned out the crumpled dollar bills and loose

Winnie Mae

change onto Mr. Farsee's glass counter, thinking that this one was going to be different.

"Here you are, young man, and I wish you most sincerely good flying weather," said Mr. Farsee.

The boy was mesmerized. The box was as light as air, and only a faint rustling of balsa wood and paper told him there was really a model airplane inside. The outside of the box was covered with the

Winnie Mae

most beautiful drawings of the plane in flight, and the side panels were full of information about the history of the real "Winnie Mae."

That night, after being released from the dinner table, the boy made a beeline for his workshop in the basement. His dad had cleared a section of his workbench for him, and it had become increasingly congested with stacks of model boxes and plans and bits and pieces of projects underway. He sometimes would draw pictures at the workbench or put linseed oil on his catcher's mitt; it was that kind of place. The boy cleared a spot and settled in. He gently opened the wondrous box and examined the contents.

After looking at the parts and reading through the plans, the boy could tell there was something strange about the model. "Dear customer, We welcome your desire to remember flying and have designed the Winnie Mae to meet that intent. By following the practice of this construction closely, we hope you shall attain the realization of your truest dreams." The boy decided the instructions might be a crude translation of some exotic foreign language because there were other marks and symbols on the plans that didn't look familiar either.

Winnie-Mae

Also, many of the instructions were just plain odd. The boy noticed that several steps in the building process had to be done at certain times of day. The wings had to be built after dinner on a night with a new moon. The propeller was to be sprinkled with drops of water from a pond with sunfish in it. The wheels had to be attached at dawn, and the glue for the tires and landing gear had to have a pinch of garden dirt mixed in.

Winnie Mae

The instructions for building the rudder read: "Direction is determined by grace and will working in concert." The Ford Tri-motor was a walk in the park compared to this.

At times as he was building it, he would come down and find a section of wing finished or a decal attached, but he couldn't remember doing it. The closer the boy got to completing the project, the more convinced he became that the Winnie Mae was more than just a rare model kit. The plans talked about believing in what you create, or creating what you believe, he wasn't quite sure which.

When he leaned back from the completed model for the first time, he thought it would be easy to believe in the Winnie Mae. It was so magnificent. It sat on his workbench as if sitting on some runway long ago, fueled up and waiting for takeoff at dawn.

The next morning the boy placed the Winnie Mae on the lazy Susan in the middle of the breakfast table. He spun the platter slowly, proudly pointing out various details to his parents. He told them about its 450-horsepower engine, and how the pilot only had one eye, and how fast it flew. The boy told them about the weird instructions, and

Winnie Mae

Winnie Mae

the dreams he'd had, seeing the Winnie Mae flying, with crowds waving and cheering as she took off. His parents seemed to be losing interest, so he tried to talk faster. He had so much to tell them. He didn't even get to the part about suspecting the model was some kind of magic kit, because they had to leave to go shopping. His mom said that his dreams didn't surprise her at all, and that actually it was curious he wasn't marching around with a silk scarf and a flying helmet on.

The boy watched the station wagon back out of the driveway and head off to town. They were good parents, and he knew they were doing their best. But when it came to things like magic and model building and dreams and such, he was on his own. They never took any of the really important stuff seriously. All they talked about was work and following rules. But he had a feeling that his parents had been different once.

He held the airplane at arm's length as he walked out the driveway, sunlight touching the wings for the first time. He made his way between the neighbors' houses across the street, cutting across

Winnie-Mae

Winnie Mae

Farmer Hoxsie's field. Then he crested the hill of his own private meadow: it was a perfect place for tank battles, test flights, any kind of daydreaming.

In the cool shade of an ancient tree, the boy lay in the soft grass, his head propped on his knapsack. He held the Winnie Mae up against the brilliant blue sky. Puffballs of cumulus clouds drifted past, giving the sensation of motion to the little model. He heard the sound of an old airplane droning along in the distance. The noise was faint, but it sounded familiar. The boy pretended the sound was coming from the Winnie Mae's engine. He could almost see the fine spray of oil and soot on the fuselage from the exhaust. The sound seemed to get closer, louder. He rubbed his eyes and looked around.

He was inside the cabin of the airplane! Several hundred feet below, he could see the meadow and his favorite tree! As the airplane banked gently left, he realized he had just thought of going left. He thought to climb, the engine increased power and the plane began to lift. He imagined turning to the right, and the big plane rolled gracefully over into a right bank, the horizon sweeping past.

Winnie-Mae

It was wonderful to fly! The boy settled in and decided to follow his path home. He had never seen his favorite haunts from the air before, and in the cool morning blues and greens of summer, everything looked so perfect from above. The walk that he had made so many times became a patchwork quilt like those his mother made from scraps of cloth. He recognized his house immediately, the white clapboards blazing in the morning sun. He flew over low enough to

discover a bird's nest in the top branches of the maple tree next to his bedroom window.

He decided to head over to the fishing hole. Long purple shadows cast by houses and trees crossed over carpets of green. He picked up the meandering line of the stream leading to the bridge and dropped down to treetop level. As the stone bridge filled his windshield, he could see the old men waving their hats as he roared past. The boy decided to make another pass. He leveled out and added full power, and just as he flashed past the bridge, he snap-rolled the Winnie Mae completely around in a dazzling victory roll!

Next thing he knew he was sitting up in the grass of the meadow, rubbing his eyes. His head had slipped off the knapsack and bumped the ground. The sun was level with the ridge of the hill to his left, and that meant he was very late for supper. The boy quickly gathered up the Winnie Mae and set off at a run for home.

The boy was afraid to tell his parents what had happened, but he had to tell somebody about his amazing adventures. So the next morning, he set off with the Winnie Mae under his arm to tell the fish-

Winnie Mae

ermen. They wouldn't laugh at him, and besides, he wanted to know if they'd seen the Winnie Mae yesterday. He held the little plane up as he walked along, watching its shadow ripple across the grass. He imagined the ground was the ocean and the plane was skimming the surface of the Atlantic on its solo journey.

The boy was distracted and didn't pay attention to where he was going. Normally, he avoided walking past the grange because older boys hung out there, and some of them didn't seem to like him. The boy was generally looked on with suspicion as there wasn't a model builder among them. The older boys took after their fathers, who frowned upon daydreaming and tinkering. So, when Billy Saunders stepped out and asked him what he was coddling under his arm, he felt his heart leap up into his throat.

It could have been worse, he told himself later. After taunting him and pushing him around, the boys focused their attention on destroying the Winnie Mae. It didn't take all that long to undo so much. They tore its wings off and stamped the fuselage into tattered bits. They handed him the remains of his beloved model plane and left him standing there, crying. He felt so ashamed to be crying, and yet he was overwhelmed.

The Winnie Mae would not fly again. The magic that enabled him to do so much was gone forever. The boy continued in the direction of the bridge. It wasn't far and the fishermen would understand.

The old men were very kind to the boy. They helped him to a comfortable spot in the shade, and cotton swabs and Band-Aids appeared

Winnie Mae

Winnie-Mae

from their tackle boxes. He was given a Thermos mug of tea, and his model's remains were examined with tremendous respect.

Aldous Johnson spoke up. "Well, son, it may not seem like it, but those fellas were just doin' their part. We all feel bad about the Winnie Mae, son. Don't get us wrong. We loved your fly-by the other morning, it's just that we're much more happy that your real flying lessons are about to begin, if you're ready that is." His eyes crinkled up playfully and he leaned back on his heels, waiting for the boy's reply.

"Then you guys really saw me fly?" the boy asked.

"Of course, son, and that wasn't a half-bad victory roll either."

The boy was thrilled to know that the fishermen had actually seen the Winnie Mae. "Oh, Mr. Johnson, isn't there any way to fix her? The kit really was magic, wasn't it? I knew it had special powers and I followed every one of the directions."

Aldous sat down next to the boy and the others gathered round. "We think you're ready, son, to learn the real secret of that model kit you built. You may not realize it right now, but all around us people

Winnie-Mae

Winnie Mae

are getting opportunities to believe. You happened to get yours in a model airplane kit. Your chance came a whole lot sooner than ours, and that's why we're so happy for you. You were ready and the message came to you."

"What message, Mr. Johnson? What are you talking about?"

"Flying, son. The Winnie Mae was a reminder made especially for you. The crazy instructions and all that mumbo-jumbo, well that just helped things along a bit, made it possible for you to believe. You might say it freed you up so as you could let your imagination soar."

The other men chuckled a bit among themselves and the boy was hurt that they seemed to be laughing at him.

"I thought you understood, but I guess no one really does. The Winnie Mae was magic. I don't care what you say." The boy snatched up the remains of his beloved model and set off for home. The fishermer were just senile old duffers after all. Nobody understood the Winnie Mae's magic except him.

His parents looked over his cuts and bruises and carefully gathered what was left of the Winnie Mae and put it in a box, high on a shelf in the living room. The boy felt hollow inside and had no more interest in the little plane anyway. It had all been a dream and he was feeling confused about how it had seemed so real at the time.

Over the next few weeks, the boy hardly ventured down to his workshop, except to retrieve his catcher's mitt. He sometimes thought of the Winnie Mae, but only to remind himself of how childish it was to waste his time daydreaming.

Then one day his father and mother were joking around after lunch. His mom was ribbing his dad, "When your father was a boy, I have been told on good authority that he, too, was quite the daydreamer. Even built a model or two, isn't that right, Arnold?"

The boy's father ruffled his paper, pretending not to hear. "Whatever you say, Hon. I'm sure it's all true, even if I can't remember."

The boy went for a walk that afternoon, thinking about what the fishermer had said about believing. Maybe all grownups went through this and just forgot.

It was a perfect afternoon for wandering, and the boy was comfortable letting his thoughts roam as he headed off. It was hard to

Winnie·Mae

picture his dad building models and daydreaming. Out of habit, the boy followed his old path, the one to the dreaming tree. He picked the occasional bramble or branch of honeysuckle out of the way and marveled at how much things had grown. As he made his way along, the boy realized that it was only his regular passage through the woods that kept the trail open.

He found his favorite spot exactly the same. The tree and meadow

Winnie Mae

looked like the perfect place to rest. He lay down and let his thoughts fall away, one after another. The beautiful blue of the sky, so deep and steady, was all he saw. The boy relaxed and felt that delicious tingling sensation you sometimes get right before you fall asleep. He thought at first an insect was buzzing around his ear. But when he focused on the sound, it got louder and more distinct.

The boy rubbed his eyes, and sat up to look around. He was astonished to find himself peering through the windshield of the Winnie Mae, looking down at the meadow below! Of course the sound was familiar, it was the old plane's massive engine! He was overjoyed to be flying again!

It was a calm afternoon, and the sky was clear except for an occasional cotton puff of cloud drifting past. The Winnie Mae climbed higher, and the horizon opened out in all directions. The boy pressed close to the glass, looking at the light reflecting off the ocean hundreds of miles to the east.

He thought of the fishermen and how grateful he was for their kindness. He thought of his mom and dad, and how much they loved him,

Winnie・Mae

and the next thing he knew the Winnie Mae was banking gently to the left, turning toward home. The boy could easily see his house off in the distance, and he noticed two bright specks in the yard. His parents were out back gardening. The Winnie Mae's shadow rippled across the treetops, and it reminded the boy of when he would walk along with the Winnie Mae held out at arm's length—its shadow following the contours of the ground.

Then the boy remembered all that had happened in the last month, and he became afraid. The magical model had been destroyed and yet he was flying! For a moment he began to doubt that all this was really possible, and as the jokes and taunting of the boys who had destroyed the Winnie Mae sounded in his mind, the engine coughed. It caught the boy's attention; the engine had never once missed a beat. As the boy looked down at the Winnie Mae's shadow, he thought of how impossible this was, how no grownup would believe it. The engine sputtered again, and as the boy watched, the shadow of the Winnie Mae flickered, nearly disappearing.

In that moment, he felt the coolness of the grass he was lying on and the quiet breeze of the meadow ruffling his hair. The boy thought back to what the fishermen told him. Grownups know, but forget. They said the model kit was a "reminder" just for him.

The boy suddenly realized that without the Winnie Mae, he wouldn't have allowed for the magic of possibility. Just then, his parents' faces turned upwards, squinting into the sun. The sound of the old plane's engine had caught their attention. The boy realized the magic was in his choice, and with that he dipped the wings of the Winnie Mae in greeting as he soared past into the blue of the afternoon sky.

Copyright © 1998 by H.B. Lewis
Designed by Rita Marshall

All rights reserved. No part of this publication may be reproduced or
transmitted in any form or by any means, electronic or mechanical, including
photocopy, recording, or any information storage and retrieval system,
without permission in writing from the publisher.

Requests for permission to make copies of any part of the work should be mailed to:
Permissions Department, Harcourt Brace & Company, 6277 Sea Harbor Drive,
Orlando, Florida 32887-6777.

The Rumi poem is from *The Essential Rumi*, originally published by
Threshold Books, 139 Main Street, Brattleboro, Vermont 05301

Creative Editions is an imprint of
The Creative Company, 123 South Broad Street, Mankato, Minnesota 56001.

Library of Congress Catalog Card Number: 98-84159   ISBN: 0-15-201954-5

First edition
A C E F D B
Printed in Italy

STILL POINT

FOLLOW THROUGH

FUSELAGE ASSEMB
NOTE: CUT SWIFTLY
AND DECISIVELY BUT
WITH COMPASSION